OLIVIA™
and the Pet Project

adapted by Lauren Forte
based on the screenplay "Olivia's Pet Project"
written by Matt Negrete
illustrated by Jared Osterhold

Ready-to-Read

Simon Spotlight
New York   London   Toronto   Sydney   New Delhi

Based on the TV series OLIVIA™ as seen on Nickelodeon™

SIMON SPOTLIGHT
An imprint of Simon & Schuster Children's Publishing Division
1230 Avenue of the Americas, New York, New York 10020
First Simon Spotlight edition February 2015
OLIVIA™ Ian Falconer Ink Unlimited, Inc. and © 2015 Ian Falconer and Classic Media, LLC
For information about special discounts for bulk purchases, please contact Simon & Schuster Special Sales at
1-866-506-1949 or business@simonandschuster.com.
Manufactured in the United States of America 0115 LAK
1 2 3 4 5 6 7 8 9 10
ISBN 978-1-4814-2896-5 (hc)
ISBN 978-1-4814-2895-8 (pbk)
ISBN 978-1-4814-2897-2 (eBook)

Olivia takes Perry
for a playdate
with Mrs. Buttercup.

"Perry teaches
Mrs. Buttercup bad habits,"
says Daisy.

"I do not want her to play with Perry anymore."

Olivia tells her mom
about Perry.
"Perry must learn to
behave," says Mom.

"You will figure out something."

Later, Francine and
Gwendolyn walk by.
Perry is still misbehaving.

"Gwendolyn behaves so well," says Olivia. "She went to charm school," says Francine.

"I will open my own charm school," says Olivia.

"First we will practice table manners," says Olivia. "Perry, take small, polite bites."
Perry does not obey.

Olivia wants to show
Perry how to act.
Ian puts on a dog costume.
He will model good
behavior.

"Fetch!" yells Olivia.
Ian fetches the ball.

"Fetch!" Olivia yells again.
Perry fetches the ball too!
He gets a treat.
"It worked!" cries Francine.

"Roll over," says Olivia.
Ian rolls over.

"Now you roll over," Olivia
tells Perry.
Perry rolls over.
"Good dog!" says Olivia.
Perry gets another treat.

Ian burps.

"Excuse me," he says.

"I mean, 'Woof.'"

"You are now a charm
school graduate,"
Olivia tells Perry.

Olivia and Perry visit Daisy
again. Mrs. Buttercup has
ruined the garden.
The Prettiest Garden
contest is today!

Olivia has an idea.
She tells Perry to fetch
the paper flowers from her
house. Perry obeys.

The judges love the garden!
"It is more than a garden.
It is art!" they say.

"Can our dogs have playdates now?" asks Olivia. "Yes, I am so happy that I won!" cheers Daisy.

Mom tells Olivia that she did a great job training Perry. "Now I want to train Perry to fetch my doll!" says Olivia.